Ron Mueller

Border Crosser

Ron Mueller

The Problem Solver 3:
Border Crossers
Ron Mueller

Around the World Publishing LLC
4914 Cooper Road Suite 144
Cincinnati, Ohio 45242-9998

This book is a work of fiction. Names, characters, places, and incidents either are products of the author's imagination or are used fictitiously. Any resemblance to actual events or locales or persons, living or dead, is entirely coincidental.

Border Crossers, by Ron Mueller © 2021

ISBN 13: 978-1-68223-173-9
ISBN 10: 1-68223-173-9

Distributed by Ingram
Cover Picture by Bruce Rolff @Dreamstime
Cover Design by Ron Mueller

To all the people

seeking a better life

in one of the best countries in the world

Table of Content

<u>Introduction</u>

It is a troubled world. The human species has, like no other, risen to dominate the world. The rise is marked with amazing beauty and grace. It is also marked by cruelty to other humans and a disregard for the negative impact they have on their only home, the earth.

The beauty found in poetry and writing, the beauty found in paintings and sculptor is more than countered by the wars, the intentional environmental destruction, and the barriers each separate country imposes on its peoples and the neighboring states.

The belief of limited resources, the behavior of greed, the desire for wealth and the desire for control are all factors in the behavior exhibited by those who surface at the top of the heap. The ability of various leaders, in a myriad of areas, to convince those more interested in their immediate family well-being allows those interested in domination to rise to positions of influence and power. Often their belief is that they have been ordained to be in charge or alternately they are smarter and should be in the lead.

The rise of the rule of law has created a situation where fairness is managed by laws developed by the representatives of the people. Even in the situation found in the United States that has three branches of government designed to maintain the system of fairness to all, slavery, and women's right to vote were initially missed. More recently the rights of gay or lesbian people are in question.

Human greed, cruelty, misbehavior, and disregard of the environment seems to increase asymptotically with the rapid rise of the population.

Justice is not always served. This situation is managed by a secret organization that funds and directs the actions of ***The Problem-solver***. This is a person whose principles, judgement, behavior, and actions guide him in how to resolve problems that otherwise would be left unchecked.

The problems are many. The problems are anywhere in the world. The problems are solved in the best manner that The Problem-solver determines.

See if you agree with the problem resolutions, that this Problem-solver, ***Ian Sinclair***, has chosen for his various assignments.

<u>Chapter 1: Border Crosser</u>

Ian watched as the news camera zoomed in on the back of a panel truck. It had been found by the Arizona highway patrol abandoned in the hot summer Arizona sun. The temperature had reached an ungodly one hundred thirteen degrees.

The truck was filled with more than thirty bodies. It was clear by how they were piled up trying to scale the interior wall that the occupants had used their hands or a boot trying to break out. Ian was sure that to the last the occupants desperately shouted, cried, and pleaded. The backdoor was bent, and one occupant had broken his leg and the bone was exposed in a grotesque angle. The hands with their fingernails ripped back clearly indicated to Ian the final desperate efforts to claw their way out.

Ian absorbed the scene as the camera pulled to a distant view and then zoomed in on a mother cradling a young girl and boy to her chest. The three seemed to be in a Cinderella sleep just waiting to wake up.

The reporter walked away with a cloth over his nose as he commented about the stench of death. Some bodies were already beginning to bloat. There seemed to be an even mix of men, women, and children. It was clear to Ian that this had been mostly family units trying to get into the US.

The woman holding her children to her chest became the focus of the reporting. The report was picked up by all the national news channels and it went viral on the personal chat sites. The picture went viral with multimillion hits in just one evening.

Ian let out a groan when he heard a national news caster say, "We need action to be taken against those trafficking in across the border people smuggling. We especially need someone to take action against smugglers that abandon people in locked trailers." This was clearly a message for him to act. He was the problem-solver.

Ian watched several other major channels and listened to the same message. There was no doubt. The message could not have been clearer.

Ian left the grand family room. It was the place where he spent the early morning with a cup coffee and listened to Morning Joe before tuning in on BBC, CNN and then going on to Fox. He liked to keep a balanced perspective on what was being watched by the rest of the world. So much of what was presented as news was actually biased opinion by one side of the political aisle or the other. The worst of the group seemed to be Fox

Ian went down the hallway to his study.

He walked in and took in the book lined shelves along the two side walls of what had originally been a home library but over the years had become his office. The mahogany desk with a black three-foot-wide all in one computer faced the rear window overlooking the tennis court and the lawn around it. The Library was where he spent many hours doing research.

Ian booted up the computer and began his search on the topic of smuggling people.

After a moment he opened the bottom left hand desk drawer and extracted a locked box from the very back. He opened and picked up an older phone that did not have GPS as a function. He slowly dialed a well memorized number. It was immediately answered. He was sure the person on the phone had been expecting the call.

"Send me everything you have on smuggling people across the Mexican border. Set me up as an FBI agent with orders to go to Arizona. Give me the name of the field agent that manages that area. Arrange for me to get there in two days. And thank you," Ian said as politely as possible.

Early in his career as the problem-solver he had tried to be friendly, but he was soon calibrated on the fact that the people on the other end of the line were to remain anonymous. Whoever they were and however many made up his support team was unknown to him. He had envisioned a large work area all full of people doing his bidding and he had also envisioned a gray-haired old lady with coke bottle bifocals sitting in a darkened closet like office.

He would probably never know. All he cared about was that his support team always delivered what he needed.

The requested material began coming in almost immediately. They must have anticipated his request. He reviewed the information from past reports on the smuggling and movement of those coming across the border.

He learned of an earlier abandoned truck full of people. It had not made the news. The fact that two trucks had been abandoned in the last two months seemed to indicate carelessness, disregard or of an increased pressure by local law enforcement.

Smugglers always preferred to remain anonymous. Getting caught was their greatest fear. Subsequent publicity meant exposure and scrutiny, so their bosses were as likely to kill them as anyone.

The US border patrol preferred to keep the media at arms-length.

Ian looked up the local law enforcement officers in Phoenix. Phoenix was where the Highway Patrol, the Local county sheriff and the FBI regional offices were located.

He reviewed the background and assignments of the local FBI Phoenix office chief. He seemed to have a well-rounded background including a stint in the Army. He appeared to be a solid individual with personal integrity.

The human smugglers had to get past the security, monitoring and patrolling done by Homeland Security. In fact, the border patrol and the Homeland Security organization were highly trained and highly motivated. Ian's assessment was that they were good at their jobs. He also suspected that some of them must be part of the smuggling operation.

The local sheriffs and State Highway Patrol seemed to be vigilant in their efforts to intercept the cars and truck involved in the smuggling. They seemed to focus on looking for those being smuggled.

Ian suspected that there were a few bad actors in these organizations that would cause the good side to get a black eye. He was certain that there was one or more bad apples in the local law enforcement agencies.

He listed the way people could be crossing the border and not getting caught.

There could be participation by local law enforcement personnel. There could be a group of border guards that would look the other way. In all cases it appeared that those doing the smuggling had help on the US side of the border.

Ian knew he needed to go to the field and get firsthand knowledge to understand the true situation.

He had already asked for his FBI persona to be reactivated. He was Herman A. Lunquist senior FBI investigator.

Ian reviewed his past history as Herman. It had continued to be updated and he laughed about some to the compliments and his high work evaluations. Someone on his support team was having a good time fabricating and building his history.

He had many personalities on record but only a few got reactivated as often as Herman. For his Journey into Russia, he had become a naturalist. In taking care of the Three Bad Pennies, he had become a cameraman. This was a natural build because he had taken on the role of a cameraman on a team of National Geographic photographers out to document the Elephant Ivory trade plight. For fighting the Pirates off the coast of Africa he had become a sailboat captain.

Ian let Lesley know that he had an upcoming business trip out west. She immediately knew what kind of business and as always gave him a kiss on the cheek and told him to be careful. Over the years Lesley had come to accept the fact that Ian would remain a problem-solver for most of his life. She constantly reminded him that they had the small fortune most people dreamed of having.

Ian gave her a hug and thanked her for loving him.

Herman Lundquist had a high status as an FBI agent. He had called Mike Lancaster the local FBI branch manager, Mike had agreed to meet him at the airport and escort him to the local FBI office.

As he came to the end of the concourse and walked out of the security area Ian spotted Mike almost immediately. Mike was roughly six two with dark hair cut almost in a short military style. Ian put him in the handsome category and thought he could have starred in the movie Men in Black.

Ian could tell that Mike was nervous and probably wondering why he, a senior FBI investigator was there. In the car on the way to the office Ian explained that he had been sent to work with Mike because the FBI hierarchy was feeling pressure about the fact that two loads of people had died in the back of trucks and there seemed to be no solution in stopping it.

Mike thanked Ian for clarifying his presence and that he could see the reason he had been sent. He wondered what Ian was going to do.

The FBI office was in the local Federal building in the heart of downtown Phoenix.

On their way up from the basement parking lot, Mike informed Ian that an office had been arranged for him and that they would share Mary Gems as their secretarial support.

They approached Mary's desk where Mike introduced Ian.

After some small talk and asking about her family, Ian asked if she would set up breakfast or lunch meetings with the leaders of the Highway Patrol, the Sheriff's office, and the Homeland Security Leader.

Ian made the point that he wanted his meetings to be on an informal basis. He did not want formality to become a barrier. He wanted everyone to know him on a more personal basis and feel somewhat relaxed around him.

Mary agreed to do so but made the point that the Homeland Security Leader was located in a small town about two hours away.

Mike next led Ian to an office next to his.

Ian commented that he hoped not to be at the desk at all.

Next Mike walked to a small room with a coffee pot, a shelf full of cups, a small refrigerator and stainless-steel sink.

"This is as good as it gets here in the office. If you want something better, May's restaurant just down the street makes a great breakfast and lunch and serves a variety of soft drinks, iced tea as well as great cup of coffee," Mike fired off in rapid order.

Ian could tell that Mike was still nervous.

He had a good feeling about Mike. He could see them working well together.

Ian followed Mike out of the coffee room

He asked Mike to bring him up to date on the investigation of the deaths of the people found in both of the abandoned panel trucks.

Mike said that the trucks were registered to two separate local truck rental companies. The rental companies had contracts on file for the trucks and everything was in order. The persons renting the trucks and their driver license information were fake.

The FBI was working with the state and states around to see if they could determine who the drivers might have been. The trail at this moment was cold.

The records of the companies were being reviewed to determine how many other times a truck had been rented under a fictitious name. The net had been cast wider and truck rentals from all rental companies were being scrutinized.

Mike commented that it would take time to get through this investigation.

Ian commented on the impressive and solid approach Mike was pursuing. He went on to describe how great it would be if the two of them solved this current case and put an end to trucks being abandoned.

He asked Mike to speculate what action he would take if he could take any action he wanted. What would he do?

There was a soft knock on the door just as Mike was about to answer. Mary opened the door and informed them that she had set up breakfasts for the next three days for the two of them.

Ian thanked Mary and she closed the door.

He then suggested that he and Mike continue their discussion over lunch.

Mike led the way to May's. He said that he recommended the Reuben special.

After lunch Mike dropped him off at the downtown Hampton Inn.

Ian checked in and went up to his room. After a long shower, he sat down and turned on his computer and thoroughly reviewed the information he had on each of the law enforcement leaders.

Mathew Martin was the leader of the highway patrol. In his mid-fifties Mathew had served in the Marines. He had a wife and three children, all now in their late teens and early twenties. He had an impressive record and had quickly risen in the states highway patrol organization. It made no sense to Ian that he would be involved.

Bill Peters was the local sheriff. He too had the same family profile. He had an Army background and had been elected sheriff four times. He was known for his active participation in getting downtown Phoenix renovated and well-lit, so people could safely enjoy their time in the city.

It made no sense to Ian that either these two would be involved.

He did not rule out someone in their organizations.

The next morning, he walked to May's diner. The appealing smell of fresh rolls, bacon and was trumped by the smell of coffee. As the waitress poured his coffee it immediately captured Ian's mind and made his stomach growl. He sat down and looked around. He had arrived early, so he could watch the customers come in.

Someone in a dark blue city police uniform with a gold badge on the chest came in and sat in a far corner booth. A moment later a person in a tan uniform with State Highway Patrol embroidered where the sleeves met the shoulder came in and joined the person in the corner. They both looked over at Ian.

Ian took in the two seasoned, well-aged older men sitting in full uniform at the booth. He stood and walked over and introduced himself. He had planned to meet first with the highway patrol leader, but it was clear they had talked to each other. The Highway Patrol leader introduced himself as Mathew Martin and then introduced the City Police Chief, Bill Peters.

Mathew said he preferred to be called Matt, said that the two had talked and decided that they would meet the investigating FBI leader together.

Ian thanked them for having breakfast with him.

At that moment Mike walked in and came over to the table. He apologized for being late.

Ian noted that Mike seemed to be treated as one of them.

Ian was the odd one out and was the one they all seemed to be wondering about. He surprised the group by asking about their families and the age of their kids. He had the statistics of each family, but he was interested in listening to how each of the people at the table related to their family.

The discussion that followed made it clear to him that "Matt" and Bill were old and good friends. He made note that these were family men, proud of their work and solid in their integrity. This made it easier for Ian. If there was corruption in their organization, it would involve those below these two. The problem would be deeper in the organization, but he would not be fighting the organization leaders.

After breakfast, Ian accompanied by Mike went on tour of the border and to the office of border security to see how they operated.

The drive to the office of border security took over an hour. Ian used this time to get to know Mike. He listened as Mike described coaching his two sons in soccer, baseball, and basketball. Mike did not want his sons to play football.

They arrived at the Homeland Security office and met with Ricard Butterfield the regional director. Rick as he wanted to be called showed Ian a map and the way the area was patrolled. He invited Ian on a drive through tour along the border.

Ian gladly accepted. Rick led the way to a large, air-conditioned trail buggy and for the rest of the day he, Mike and Rick drove the route that his border guards patrolled. It didn't take Ian long to figure out that the guys in the field needed directions from the drones that flew overhead.

They and their dogs made great teams. The dog handlers all took to Ian once their dogs allowed Ian to scratch them behind their ears. Their dogs showed them that Ian was OK. They commented that Ian was one of a handful of people that the dogs accepted.

Ian laughed and replied that his wife thought he was a dog too.

The team described how they went about their normal daily patrol. Their manner was professional, thorough, and very conscientious.

After learning about how the field teams were guided, Ian asked to tour the drone control office and understand how they interacted with the ground team.

Rick said the tour would need to be the next day around noon. He was joining Matt and Joe for his usual midweek breakfast at May's. He asked whether Mike would be there.

Mike answered in the affirmative and looked at Ian to see what his response would be.

Ian answered that he wouldn't miss it.

The next day after breakfast Mike and Ian followed Rick back to the Border Patrol offices. Rick led the way in and walked Ian and Mike through the normal observation shift and the communication with the border patrol vehicle surveillance and the dog patrol teams. It was clear the drone handlers had the best vantage point to see almost everything. A mole on this team could easily provide the information that would misdirect those on the ground.

On the drive back, Ian asked Mike to check on the background of all the drone operators.

Ian again guided the conversation to Mike and his family.

Mike described his home as strategically located between the Desert View Middle School, where his youngest son and middle daughter attended and the Sunny Slope High school where his oldest son was now in his junior year.

The family Church was just beyond the middle school. The family doctor was located across from the High School and a hospital was just a stone's throw north of the high school.

He and his wife belonged to a health club less than three miles away. Mike described it as a convenient arrangement for the family.

He had a large two story, five-bedroom home on a corner lot that faced third street and was blessed with a dead-end street to its right.

Mike made a point of mentioning the nine-foot interior ceilings that kept the air conditioning bill reasonable. He liked the fact that the large size of the house and the relatively small size of the lot which made the yard work reasonably easy.

Mike extended an invitation to Ian to a family grill out. He explained the grilling would happen out in the backyard, but everyone would be taking shelter in the air-conditioned back patio.

Ian said he would love to meet his family and looked forward to the grill out.

Ian spent Saturday sleeping in late, taking a swim and working out. He took in a movie and spent some time reviewing the case.

Sunday morning early Ian took a walk-through downtown Phoenix. The heat of the day was building when he flagged down one of the few cabs and gave him Mike's address.

The grill out and meeting the family put Ian in a good mood. Then toward the end of the day Mike received a call. He beckoned Ian over and quietly shared the fact that the border patrol had lost a large group of border crossers but had seen a light grey or perhaps dirty white panel truck leaving the area.

Ian and Mike agreed to skip the Monday breakfast and meet early in the office and figure out what to do.

That evening Ian began to study the routes that he would choose if he were transporting illegal aliens and wanted to minimize his chances of getting caught. Based on the mileage of each of the two confiscated trucks that had been previously used Ian plotted various routes. He decided to check these routes with Matt and Bill at breakfast on Monday morning.

Ian met Mike at the office and suggested that they have breakfast at Mays. He had questions for both Bill and Matt.

Mike was especially interested in Ian's study on possible travel routes and wondered why his team had not done something similar.

Ian pointed out that he had no clue about travel in the region, but he didn't know what else to do so he was doing what he always did best. He created his own sandbox to play in and hoped there was no cat shit in it.

There seemed to be one route that best fit the miles. It also ended just shy of Interstate 40, which was a main East-West traffic corridor. Ian had used a red pen to trace Highway 80 north, to 75, to 78, to 180 then on to 32, 36 and finally 117. This brought both trucks very close to Interstate 40. It was a slow tedious route, but it certainly kept the trucks off the main thoroughfares.

Ian figured that it was probably around this area where a transfer to other modes of transport would be made. The second leg could be many via separate transports. There were endless dispersal scenarios that Ian could think of.

Matt and Bill concurred on the route Ian liked best. They figured it was as good as any and asked what good knowing this would now do for those who had died.

Ian agreed that it did nothing for them, but he felt it might help to be ready for the next time. And he pointed out that Rick had let Mike know on Sunday that a white panel truck had left the border.

Ian decided to drive and feel out the route he had mapped. He figured his chances were very low of finding anything, but the drive would occupy him and give him time to decide on the next steps he needed to take.

He asked Mike if the office kept any cases of water handy. He asked that several cases be put in the trunk.

Mike said he would have one of his guys put it in the back of the car Ian was being issued and asked if Ian was expecting to find a truck load of people.

Ian replied that he had no clue, but he was going to be Boy Scout ready.

Ian walked out to the assigned car, checked the trunk, and threw in his small personal needs bag.

Ian left Phoenix and began what he decided was a scenic drive through the scraggly pine covered mountains surrounded by a wide skirt of sage, cactus and tumble weed stretch of barren desert. Ian encountered almost no traffic. An occasional car or truck going the opposite direction broke the otherwise monotonous drive. He was almost all the way to Interstate 40 when a white panel truck stopped on the side of the road caught his eye. He slowed down as he drove past.

He saw no one.

The truck seemed to be deserted. A red flag went up in Ian's mind. Unbelievably it was the exact scenario he had imagined.

Ian decided to go back to the truck and take a closer look. He parked just past the truck on the opposite side of the road and carefully approached the truck. He looked out to the right of the truck to see if the driver was out in that direction. The underside of the truck was clear. It seemed the truck was deserted.

Ian walked up to the cab and stepped up on the sideboard to look in.

Almost immediately there was pounding on the panels from inside the back of the truck. He walked to the back of the truck. The doors were locked.

Ian pounded on the backdoor and in Spanish he told them to wait a moment. He would open the backdoors.

The truck had a cross lug nut wrench but no straight bar. Ian went to his car and came back with the hockey stick style lug wrench most cars carry. The lock was a standard case quarter inch shank. It snapped on his first hard twist.

A swoosh of hot air from inside hit him as the doors came open. Ian was almost overwhelmed by the smell of sweat and urine. He was immediately angered by these conditions. The relief of finding everyone alive was the only thing that placated Ian.

The people inside needed help and they needed water. Ian knew that his earlier premonition that caused him to ask for the two cases of water now confirmed why he was still alive today. He always seemed to have these premonitions.

Ian passed the water out and told everyone to drink slowly so they would not be sick.

He got everyone out and had them sit in the shade of the truck.

Ian saw a white van approaching slowly from the direction of Interstate 40. He took a bottle of water and went to the front of the panel truck. He stood leaning against the front of the truck. The heat of the radiator added to the heat of the sun.

The oncoming van stopped about twenty feet from the truck. Two men with guns drawn got out and approached him.

They asked what the hell Ian was doing letting the people out of the truck.

Ian calmly told them to take it easy and that he had stopped to see if he could help. Ian pointed to the engine compartment. He told them that he was a mechanic in Phoenix and just happened to be driving by. Ian went on to claim that he had fixed hundreds of engines of this type and that he could help them.

The taller of the two said they would fix their own truck and Ian should just get on his way.

Ian took note that the group along the side of the truck were now standing and quietly watching. The group seemed to distract the two gunmen.

The two had finally reached the distance when Ian could go into action. He waited until the two took their next step forward.

The taller of the two took the step forward that Ian had been waiting for. Ian threw his water bottle at him and took a long step forward. He deflected the gun hand with his left hand while at the same time stepping down hard on the arch of his right foot. He kept the gunman's body between he and his partners. The final stiff finger stab to his throat took him down.

As the taller gunman was just beginning to crumble, Ian delivered a round house kick to the second gunman's temple area and followed it with a downward fist blow to his nose. The second gunman fell down on his knees holding his nose with two hands and then toppled over.

Ian quickly picked up the two guns and checked the two for any other weapons. Both were carrying hunting style knives.

Ian threw the knifes back to the on looking crowd.

He asked the on lookers to take off the men's boots and pants and to throw them both into the back of the truck.

Ian was surprised by the energy and enthusiasm the crowd displayed as they picked the two up and took off the articles Ian had specified. They literally threw them into back of the truck. There was a cheer when the doors were shut.

Ian would interrogate the two but first he had to disperse the people that were now looking to him for guidance.

Chapter 2: Border Crosser – Imelda

Elisa lay against her mother's side. She was hot and thirsty. She and her mother had been riding in the absolute black darkness in the back of a truck for a very long time. The truck started jerking and then stopped.

When they had first jumped into the truck Elisa had been happy because they had escaped the patrol dogs. Her friends had told her the dogs ripped people apart and ate them. But now she was hot, thirsty, and was really scared. She could not even see her mother's face, and it smelled really bad. She kept her head on her mother's chest and listened to her heartbeat. Her mother kept praying and singing which really worried Elisa.

Imelda hugged her daughter. The heat was unbearable. They had not been given any water or provisions. She and the others in the group that were in the truck with her had crossed the border into the US during the night. Their guide had led them across the river. They had come through a hole cut in a fence and then jogged for about a half mile to where the truck was waiting for them.

Imelda had to drop all her belongings and pick up Imelda so the two of them would not be left behind. They had all jumped into the back of the truck and the doors were shut. It was hot, and the ride was bumpy and bruising until they reached what must have been the highway. Then it was a long monotonous ride in the pitch black.

The heat and the bad smell seemed to go up together. She hugged Elisa to her chest and said a quite prayer.

She was on the way to meet her husband in Cincinnati, Ohio. He told her he had a small place to live and was working for the state as a gardener in a local state hospital. They had agreed it was time for her to bring Elisa and come live with him.

Now as she sat in the back of the truck she wondered if their lives back in Oaxaca had been all that bad. Carlos and she had been friends since they were kids. Their families lived on adjacent small farms and did fairly well. They grew most of their own food and raised a few goats and sheep. Their chickens provided eggs and meat.

It was a simple life. It was a good life for a poor family. But it held little hope that the future would be any different than the past.

The two had married shortly after getting out of high school. Carlos went to work for a local building materials supplier. He got his pay partly in goods and the rest in cash.

He got permission from both of their families to build a small home on the boundary property where the two farms came together.

Carlos and Imelda had sketched out a small single story two-bedroom home. A tiled entry hall split the home with one bedroom on each side. The bathroom and shower were on the left back corner. The kitchen was the biggest room in the house and featured a large table at its center. A window over the sink looked out to the outdoor cooking area.

Every day Carlos would bring home a few bricks or bags of cement. Every weekend the two would work at building the next part of their home. It took them almost a year to build their home. The two had worked together every evening. This was a fond memory for Imelda. They had grown closer together with each brick they cemented into the wall. Each was a gold brick for their love for each other.

There was a big party to celebrate the completion of the home. They moved in and immediately they felt a new surge of hope for the future. Imelda became pregnant only a few weeks later. Her pregnancy was another cause for celebration.

The next big event was the drilling of the well and then having electricity brought to the house. Each was followed by celebration.

Life was good.

Elisa was born in December. Dark brown eyes, a full head of black hair, blessed with all her fingers and toes, she was a perfect child. It was the most joyous of times. She was their Christmas baby.

Carlos was a consummate father. Always good with his work roughened but skilled hands, he made a crib by hand for Elisa and a rocking chair for Imelda. Both were treasures Imelda cherished.

For a few years, their lives seemed to be going smoothly and making progress. Then the economy went bad. Carlos lost his job. No matter how hard he tried he could not find another.

He was despondent and had a feeling of hopelessness. Their few chickens and small garden kept them from going hungry but there was no income and they had little money in reserve. Carlos was despondent and shared his feeling of hopelessness.

A friend of Carlos told him about working in the US and how several of his friends were up north and sending money home to their families. The jobs were not hard to get and if one lived economically the money was enough to send home and to save.

Shortly afterwards Carlos made up his mind to cross the border to the US. His friend's friend lived in Cincinnati and vouched that there were abundant jobs to be had.

Carlos experienced an easy trip. His crossing went smoothly, and he quickly made his way to Cincinnati. Once he arrived, he called back home and told Imelda how easy it had been. Only the border crossing itself had been somewhat challenging and scary, but the rest of the trip was no different than taking a trip into Mexico City. His calls and a few letters shared the various part time jobs of gardening or working on small construction projects. The money he sent home was more than enough for Imelda to live on and to provide some extras for Elisa.

Life on the farm was again good but Carlos was missing.

When he landed a permanent job, he asked her to come to Cincinnati. He felt the US offered a better chance for their family to get ahead. Elisa would get a good education and have the chance to go to college. Carlos was thinking ahead about what was good for his family.

Imelda shared her decision to go to Cincinnati with both sets of grandparents.

At first both grandparents asked her not to go. They understood the bleak future that staying in Mexico meant for Imelda, but they wanted to have their only granddaughter close at hand. All of them saw how much both Imelda and Elisa missed Carlos and they then became supportive and wished her good luck. Imelda turned down their offer of money and instead left most of what she had saved with her mother.

She and Elisa were now into their second week of travel. Elisa had been especially afraid of the border crossing. They made the crossing with a group of about twenty people made up mostly of young men. Counting herself there were four women in the group. She was the only one with a child.

When border guards seemed to approach them with dogs, their guide told them to run as fast as they could to a white panel truck waiting for them. Imelda had dropped all her belongings, so she could scoop up Elisa to keep up with the rest.

They all jumped into the truck and the doors were closed. The truck lurched forward and went speeding away. It was pitch black in the truck and everyone remained quiet. Someone with a cigarette lighter flicked it on and they all got a quick look around the empty truck. There was no water or food.

Imelda now had a new worry. She had no money, and she did not have a way get to Cincinnati.

Occasionally there were some whispered conversations. Otherwise, there was only darkness and silence.

Imelda softly hummed some of Elisa's favorite songs. They were together and soon she hoped that somehow, they would get to Cincinnati.

Then the truck sputtered and jerked and came to a stop. Everyone got ready to get out, but the doors did not open.

Fear slowly crept into Imelda's mind. She hugged Elisa to her and made a prayer to the Virgin Mary.

Someone pounded on the side of the truck. Another group kicked at the backdoor.

Imelda just kept praying.

It seemed they had been still for a very long time when suddenly the truck leaned as if someone was getting into the driver's side of the truck.

Almost everyone began pounding on the side of the truck walls and yelling at the top of their voices.

Imelda just kept repeating, "please open the door".

The rattling of the lock on the backdoor caused everyone to suddenly become silent.

Then in what Imelda considered the best bad Spanish she had ever heard; someone call out and let them know that he was going to open up the backdoor.

She knew it was not either of the two who had been driving the truck. They were Mexican and spoke perfect Spanish.

Imelda crossed her herself and thanked the Lord.

As the doors opened, the people in the back rushed out. It was hot out in the sun but there was fresh air to breathe.

Imelda led Elisa out and into the shade that was on the desert side of the truck.

She was surprised to see a total stranger, a gringo, helping them.

She watched as he went to the trunk of the car across the road. He had two young men carry two cases of bottled water across the road.

He took the first two bottles and gave it to her and Elisa.

He kept a third for himself but did not open it.

Imelda had tears in her eyes as she thanked him.

Everything went silent as a van was coming toward the front of the truck.

Imelda watched as the generous man that had opened the door went to the front of the truck. All he had was a bottle of water in his hands.

Two men got out of the truck. Imelda realized they had their guns aimed at the person that had freed her.

This time her prayer was for him.

It seemed that the person she was praying for had no idea about the danger he might be in.

Imelda moved behind the front left wheel of the truck and put Elisa behind her. She listened to what was being said.

Suddenly the man moved so swiftly that she almost missed what was happening. The two men with guns were down, moaning and bleeding. The strange man had both their guns and was asking the two be thrown into the back of the truck. He told the crowd to take of their shoes and pants before locking them in.

She was surprised to hear herself shouting when he asked for some help in throwing the two men into the back of the truck.

Imelda leaped up to help but she was pushed aside by the rush of several of the men. She suddenly realized that she did not like the two men on the ground. She had paid a lot of money and had been treated worse than a pig.

She wanted to give the stranger helping her a hug.

Imelda came back to her bleak reality. She was in trouble. She had no money. No clothes but what she had on. She was hungry, and she had a young daughter who was clinging to her in fear.

Her mind kept returning to one thought, "How was she going to get to Cincinnati?

Chapter 3: Border Crossers - Deliverance

Ian looked down the empty road toward the way he had driven out toward Interstate 40. He turned toward the Interstate and looked at another stretch of road as deserted in that direction as in the other. He had the two culprits locked in the back of the van and thirty or so people standing in the shade of the truck.

The day was coming to its peak temperature. He was sure it was more than one hundred degrees in the shade. The two in the back of the truck would already be feeling the heat. Ian would wait a little longer before he interrogated the two. They would be more willing to cooperate after exposure to the stench and to the oven like heat.

He had to disperse the border crossers. Ian was not interested in turning the group in. He inquired about who could drive the van parked in front of the panel truck. Several hands went up. Ian picked the oldest of the volunteers to do the driving.

He then asked how many were expecting rides when they got to the interstate. He noted that most of the hands were in the air.

Most notable to Ian was that the women did not raise their hands. The woman with the young girl was hanging her head.

Ian inquired about the names of the women and of the young girl. The distress in the mother's voice made it clear to Ian that she needed help.

"I am Imelda, and this is my daughter Elisa. She is turning eight this year," Imelda spoke up. I had bus tickets to go to Cincinnati, but I lost my backpack and all my belongings when we had to run for the truck. The driver of the truck was to take us to the bus stop.

Imelda's plight helped Ian make up his mind.

He told the women they would ride in his car. They should continue standing in the shade until he got the men on their way.

The men all managed to squeeze into the van. It would be a hot ride, but it was only a short distance to the Interstate. The van made a U turn and went back toward the Interstate.

Ian walked back to the car and opened all the windows. He told Imelda to sit in front with Elisa and to relax while he went and asked the two in the back of the truck a few questions.

He walked back to the truck and picked up his tire iron. He walked around to the far side and poked several holes in the side wall.

Ian asked if they were still alive. There was an immediate plea for him to let them out. Ian said that it would continue to get hotter as the sun hit its peak. If they wanted out, they would have to tell him who they worked for.

He was met with silence.

He hit the side of the truck with his tire iron and said goodbye. He wished them a good life for as long as it would last.

Ian heard one of them say it was an official in the highway patrol. They did not have a name.

Ian replied that they would not live very long if he left, and he was leaving if they did not give him a name.

"Wait, Wait, we get our orders to rent a truck and where to go over the internet. We do as instructed. We pick up the border crossers and drive to the designated location. Once the border crossers are on their way, we return the rented truck. Our pay gets transferred into our bank accounts. We never see or talk with anyone.

"How do you know it is a high-ranking official in the Highway patrol," Ian asked.

When we were first recruited the person said that he had the cover of the highway patrol at the highest level.

Ian asked for their email names and wrote them down.

He next asked if they had been the drivers of the truck found with dead people in the back. He expected the denials they gave. He would check there whereabouts later.

Ian quickly verified the email names they had given him.

He then unlatched the door and told them to get out. He told them to walk toward Interstate 40. They were to walk there and disappear from the area.

They asked for their pants and boots. Ian laughed and said that they had on what they were going to walk in.

As they began the walk the tallest one complained about his broken foot and crushed Adam's apple. The shorter one complained about his broken nose and the lump on the side of his head.

Ian replied they had met the devil and they should be happy to be alive.

Ian stood and watched them until they were at least a thousand paces down the road.

He put in a call to the Highway patrol to pick up the two men walking toward the interstate in their underwear.

He then returned to the car. He started the engine and put the air conditioner on high. Then he made a U turn and went toward the interstate.

The flashing red lights of multiple highway patrol cars surrounding the van and the men standing in a row with their hands up clearly showed the fate of the men who had driven up in the van.

Ian looked at Imelda and told her that the men would be processed, and many would be allowed to go to their US destinations. Some would be returned across the border.

Ian proceeded on and got onto the Interstate going east.

Imelda asked where Ian was taking all of them?

He replied that it would depend on what they told him. He asked for the names of the people who connected them to the border cross guides and that they tell him where they were going. He was watching the three in the back. He repeated the question in Spanish.

They all started to talk at the same time.

Ian stopped them and asked Imelda to tell her story first.

Imelda assured Ian that it was not a gangster but a family friend who knew someone who could get her connected with a border crossing guide.

Ian made it clear he was not interested in any family friends. He described the scene of a truck just like theirs but full of people who had died of the heat. They that had been discovered only a few weeks back. There was a mother, daughter and son all huddled together. They had died in her arms.

Imelda had tears in her eyes as she hugged Elisa and told him she was on the way to Cincinnati to meet her husband.

Imelda whispered thank you God. She wished she had her rosary.

Ian let her know that he would put her on a bus that would take her to her husband.

Each of the other three gave the names of their contacts in Mexico and where they were planning to go. It surprised Ian to learn that one was going to Minneapolis to meet other family members. One was on the way to Auburn, Maine to live with her best friend. And the last was on the way to Washington, DC where she had been offered a job at a local hotel.

Ian told them what was going to happen. They would spend the night at a nice hotel. They would have a pleasant evening meal at some family restaurant. He would buy each of them bus tickets to their destinations. Tomorrow they would get on their bus and make the remainder of the trip on their own

Imelda asked why he was doing this for them?

Ian explained that he did not always know why he did what he did, but he smiled and said that this time it was because Elisa smiled at him. It was so true. Ian never tried to reason why when he made these types of decisions. He figured someday he would either meet the devil or be standing at the pearly gates trying to explain his grievous sins.

Let's stop and get all of you some basic clothes to wear. Imelda, you, and Elisa go into Target and buy two outfits each and some shoes as well. Buy a small suitcase for each of you. And get anything else you need such as toothpaste and toothbrushes. Pay cash Ian said giving her enough money to cover the shopping.

"You three go separately to Sears, Kohl's and Burlington Clothes factory," Ian instructed the other three as he gave them cash as well.

Once they had departed, Ian dialed his support number and requested reservations at the Embassy Suites, the bus tickets for each of the women and cash. He asked that everything be sent to the Embassy Suites Hotel. He did not want to buy the tickets at the bus station because it would make his activities too traceable.

Ian also called into the office to let Mike know that he had been on the road driving the routes he suspected the border crossers took. He let Mike know he would be back by noon the next day.

Imelda and Elisa were the first to return. They walked toward the car pulling their very practical matching dark blue suitcases.

They were smiling and talking to each other. It was great to see the two finally relaxed and happy. Elisa was wearing her new "just do it" sneakers.

Ian had a couple of throw away phones in the glove compartment. He took one out and handed it to Imelda. Call your husband and let him know that you are safe and on the way home. Don't say anything more than that. You can tell him the whole story once you get home. You can let Elisa say hello, but she must not say anything either.

Ian could hear the happy ring in Carlos's voice as he talked to Imelda and Elisa.

Ian watched as the other three met each other on the sidewalk. They were chattering as they walked back to the car. Each had bought a different color roller board.

Ian stopped at an Olive Garden restaurant for a quick dinner. The endless salad was a hit. Everyone found something on the menu they liked. Elisa especially seemed to like the buttered bread sticks.

One of the women asked why he was being so kind. Ian replied that sometimes good things happened, and they just needed to accept it and later they should be kind to someone else. He really did not have a good answer but in his mind, he linked his actions to the much darker and deadly actions he often took when solving problems.

Ian told them that they all had room reservations at the Embassy Suites under names he had given them. They were to pay cash. You three will go first. You are sharing one room. For tonight you are Maria, Eli, and Fran.

You are friends returning from vacation. Don't talk too much. Just check in and go to the room. Enjoy a good shower and catch a movie; but stay in your room.

I will come in next and check in.

Imelda and Elisa will come in last. Your names are Angela and Justine. The two of you are on your way home.

Breakfast will be at seven on the ground floor. Enjoy your evening.

Ian moved the car to a parking space and got out, took his overnight case that he carried in the trunk and headed for the lobby.

Imelda and Elisa were on the sidewalk coming in slowly behind him.

A shower and a cup of coffee, the evening news and he was ready for bed. Ian called home and talked with Lesley and let her know all was well. Hearing her voice and listening to her tell him about her day put him at ease.

The next morning. they all met for breakfast on the first floor.

Ian had already checked out. The clerk had handed him a grey envelope that had been dropped off for him. The bus tickets and money were inside.

The five looked totally refreshed and quite local in their new clothes. It was clear by their consumption that they really enjoyed their breakfast. Ian could tell Elisa was having the time of her life.

Imelda was quiet. She was so relieved to be safe. She still found it strange to get the help that she was getting from a stranger. Her prayers had been answered.

He made sure everyone had checked out. They all enjoyed a long morning breakfast. Ian then led the way to the car. There he handed each their tickets and five twenty-dollar bills. Elisa got her own ticket and her five twenty-dollar bills.

Each said Gracias and asked how they could pay him back.

Ian told them that there was no way to pay him back but that someday they would be able to do something good for someone else. When that happened, they should do it. He told them that doing so would make them feel very good about themselves.

He knew it made him feel better.

As she got out of the car at the bus station, Elisa asked if she could write to him.

Ian would be living in the same city, but he knew that it would not be safe for him to stay in contact with her. He lied and told her that he would keep in touch with her and gave her a hug.

He got back in his car and began his drive back to Phoenix. He was going to investigate the potential that someone in the highway patrol office or the sheriff's office might be involved in the human trafficking.

In the Heart of Russia

Ian looked up the escalator leading to the luggage area and felt a surge of warmth as he saw Lesley.

Almost immediately his mood changed from the grey funk he was muddling through to a sunny, warm spring breeze feeling. Her smile was sunshine, and her hug was a furnace of warmth on a cold winter day.

When Lesley asked how his trip had gone. He simply replied that it had been very successful. And I am alive, he thought as he took her hand and led the way to pick up his luggage.

Lesley led the way to their car, and he threw his luggage into the trunk. Since he was not sure of the way back home, he took the passenger seat and Lesley drove home. Their home!

Ian was scheduled to officially start his work on the week between Christmas and New Year's Day. His HR contact had emphasized that this gave Ian a one-year head start on his health insurance and retirement benefits. His new boss agreed, so Ian spent one day in his new office before the New Year. There was one other person there and maybe a dozen in a building that normally held a thousand people.

He was a new Engineer but older than most of his coworkers and almost as old as his bosses. His experiences gave him a very different perspective. He wanted less talk and more doing. His engineering department was short staffed for the amount of work and the projects that needed staffing. His work focus and attitude served him well.

His first assignment put him in charge of modernizing a power and steam generation facility at one of the Tide manufacturing sites. Ian was glad to have the challenge of the work. Working with the project team brought him into an environment that strengthened the barrier to the dark zone of his mind.

He and Lesley were in their thirties. Lesley was worried about waiting too long to have children. Ian was a little hesitant but looked forward to being the loving dad. It was October when little Ella came into the world.

She was not only beautiful, but she also slept through the night! She smiled and gurgled. She was a happy baby.

Ian knew life was good. The Cincinnati spring was warm, and the trees grew green, and the flowers bloomed.

Ella seemed to go from diapers to walking in the blink of an eye. Her rapid progress in getting potty trained was welcome by Ian.

Then his next problem-solving assignment came to him.

A courier delivered a package to his home. Ian carried the package to the dining room table and opened it.

There was an American passport with his picture issued to Dr. Demyan Kuzmenko that immediately caught his attention. Demyan was an American Professor at the University of California. He was first generation American, born to Russian emigrants.

The enclosed documents were official Russian paperwork authorizing his travel through the tundra area to observe the condition of the wolves being released and tracked to understand the condition of the repopulation program.

The instructions also instructed him to go on vacation on the Black Sea in July.

The instructions identified the problem as a missile development program being done in the heart of Russia. The development lab was located along the Irtysh River. Ian had never heard of the Irtysh River, but he learned during research that it along with the Ob River made it the seventh longest river in the world. He learned that the river ran from China, through Kazakhstan and north through Russia to the Arctic Ocean.

During his preparation studies for the assignment, he learned about the Battle of Irtysh River fought in 657 A.D. between the Tang dynasty and the Western Turkic Khaganate. The Tang won and controlled the region.

He stopped and laughed, how could any of this historic stuff help him.

Hell, he was being sent into the land of the devil and he was learning Chinese history.

He found a travel guidebook that followed the river and gave him a better feel of the area. The vegetation along the banks of the river varied between marshlands, coniferous forests, and marshy wetlands. To his amazement the guidebook showed the warehouse district where the development lab was located. He was not absolutely sure of the specific warehouse the development facility was located but he got the lay of the river waterfront.

He made his travel arrangements.

He arranged to do a workshop in the Zwichau manufacturing plant in East Germany. This would put him a short train ride away from the Black Sea.

He would carry out his legitimate brussiness and then proceed to his problem-solving assignment.

He scheduled vacation for Demyan on a beach on the Black Sea near the town of T'bilisi.

The work session at the Zwickau plant took exactly one week. He said goodbye to the plant manager as Ian Sinclair.

He took the taxi to the train station and boarded the train to T'bilisi. He traveled into T'bilisi as Ian Sinclair but checked into his hotel as Demyan Kuzmenko.

The next day he boarded the train to Omsk. It would be a long train ride, but it would be less conspicuous than using the airlines. Omsk a beautiful city of more than one million people was one of the largest cities in Siberia.

The problem-solving assignment lay another hundred miles to the north. This was the part of the journey that was Ian's biggest concern.

He was a professor from the US studying the success or failure of the "re-wilding" effort being carried out in hopes of reducing global warming. It sounded farfetched, but it provided the cover he needed to go wandering around the wilderness. Ian had all the official paperwork to authorize his movements. He hoped his team had done a good job in making the documents look official and real.

He left Omsk on a river freighter traveling north toward Tobolsk.

The missiles were being developed in one of the local ship building plants located there. Ian would need to determine which one and then figure out how to penetrate the security that would be in place. He had no illusions about the risk.

He would "trust no one." This was his takeaway from his first assignment.

The boat ride would take him by the shipyard-warehouse thought to house the missile development program. Ian spent the slow trip upriver sketching the river side scenery. He hoped anyone watching this strange Russian American would see that he was truly interested in the landscape and the animals seen along the riverbank.

The ship's Captain stopped by several times to "practice his English" and to see how his main passenger was enjoying himself.

Ian wanted to be able to look closely at everything along the bank without being too obvious when the boat went by the shipyards. He would closely scrutinize the shipyard looking for the weak spots in the security.

The boat he was on would make a four day stop at Tobolsk to unload goods and take on additional consignments.

Ian inquired about a bed and breakfast that he might utilize while he waited for the boat to continue.

One of the riverboat crew recommended a house a few blocks from the river. Ian inquired about the price. The crewman thought it would be around a thousand rubles, maybe a little more but he said it was worth it just for the food that was offered with the room.

Ian followed the instructions of the crewman. He was sure that there was someone that would be watching but he did not sense or see anyone following him. Ian spotted the small sign for the bed and breakfast pointing inward between two multistory older homes. He followed it back to an open central courtyard.

Ian took in the neat arrangement of large, tiered pots forming a central cone four pots high and then an outside circle of pots three tiers high that filled the gaps between three sturdy benches made from three-inch-thick oak or some similar hardwood.

The older white-haired woman with a headscarf tied under her chin immediately caught Ian's eye. She looked a lot like a grandmotherly "babushka".

Ian knew little to no Russian, so he handed her the note the captain had written and in English asked if she had a room available to rent.

"You have a Russian name, but you speak English. What kind of mother would raise her son and not teach him his root language. Yes, I have a room. Follow me," she said in broken English as she gave him back the card with the ship captain's note.

You are right. I should have learned some Russian, but my mother was American, my father was Russian.

"Follow me. If you like the room you pay in advance. How long will you stay," she asked?

She wiped her hands on a wet cloth and led the way into the house.

"The boat I am on will take about four days. I only have a few days before I need to go into the wilderness to see how the wolf population is doing," Ian replied.

"You hunt wolves," she asked?

She slowly climbed the four flights of stairs to a room that was just below the roof rafters and had a window that looked out toward the courtyard. It lined up almost directly with the walkway that led to the courtyard.

"The bathroom is down one floor. It is shared by one other room. Do you want it," she asked?

"Yes, this is fine. How much," Ian asked as he put down his knapsack.

"Twelve hundred fifty ruble per day and you get a hearty breakfast," she replied.

This was within the range the sailor had mentioned. She seemed to be giving him a fair price.

He liked her attitude. She seemed to know he was not who he was trying to appear to be. He just wondered what she thought he was up to.

"Is there a simple restaurant where one can get a decent meal," Ian asked as he took out his leather bag where his money was kept?

"Tonight, I am cooking Beef Stroganov and cooked vegetables. You are welcome. The cost is two hundred rubles.

There is a sandwich store about two blocks from here and a small restaurant across the street from it. You will have to go several kilometers farther if you want anything else," she replied as she watched him take out his money.

"Let me pay you for a week. I would love to eat at your table tonight. Tomorrow I will walk around and get a feel for the neighborhood. Can I sit out in the courtyard and finish up some of the sketches I have started," Ian asked as he took out his sketch book?

"You hunt wolves, and you draw," she asked in a speculative voice and raised her eyebrows as she took the money.

 "No, I study the wolves. I draw them too. I am studying the efforts of repopulating Siberia with them. My name is Demyan," Ian said as he showed her some drawings of wolves in the wilderness.

Then he flipped to the river scenes.

"Ah, you are a strange one. You have many talents. I am sure you are also a master storyteller. I am called Raya," she said with an amused look.

"Demyan, I will call you to dinner in about an hour," she said as she turned to leave.

Ian unpacked his belongings. His camera and sketch pad were his field tools. His clothes were basic hiker's shirt and pants. His official paperwork rounded out the contents of what he carried. He was traveling light, and everything was of local make.

He had left a suitcase in the train station in Syerdlovsk with his western clothes. He would go back there after solving his problem and transform back and be a westerner on his departure.

Ian leaned out the window and studied the roof. The buildings were close enough together making it possible to get away if it proved necessary. Ian planned to look this over more closely after it got dark.

He took a change of clothes and went down to the bathroom. He hoped she provided guest towels. A quick shower, clean clothes prepared him for the evening.

He took his pencils and sketch book to the courtyard.

Ian put a few obligatory pencil strokes to the wilderness drawings. Improved a few riverside sketches and then went to the drawings of the shipyard.

Periodically, he looked up and watched Raya working in the kitchen. There didn't seem to be anyone else in the house. After dinner, he would ask about a tour of the house. He needed to get a better understanding of his surroundings.

He did a sketch of Raya doing her cooking in the kitchen. It was an eye-catching scene framed by the open door and window opening into the courtyard. Raya was focused on cutting vegetables. The sound of her knife rapidly cutting through the vegetable augmented the blur of her rapidly moving hand.

He would give the sketch he was creating, to her before he left.

Soon the great smells coming into the courtyard from the kitchen made him want to come to the table. He was eager to get inside and eat whatever Raya was cooking.

Finally, Raya came to the courtyard door and announced that it was time for dinner.

Ian closed his drawing pad and eagerly followed her in.

There were only two places set at the table.

"Yes, I have no other guests.

My husband died about six months ago. He was the one who went to the riverfront bars and recruited the men to stay at our house. It has been hard, but I will get by," Raya said as Ian sat down at the place she indicated.

Ian got an inspiration that he thought would help Raya. He would act on it tomorrow.

It would provide the perfect cover for him to wander down the waterfront.

"Would you be willing to provide breakfast and dinner for anyone just wanting to eat here," Ian asked quietly?

"Yes, for a price; just like I charged you. And if they stay here, breakfast is included but dinner is extra," Raya said firmly.

Ian showed her the picture he had drawn of her cooking in the kitchen.

"That is very good. May I have it," she said as she held the notebook in her hand.

"Yes, I will give it to you when I am done. I am going to make a series of small ones.

I will put down your address, the cost of staying here and the cost for dinner. It will invite people to eat here even if they chose not to stay.

Tomorrow, I will put them in all the bars along the river that are within reasonable walking distance," Ian said as he watched her reaction.

"Why would you do this," she asked looking suspiciously at Ian.

"Because you are Raya," Ian said.

He was playing with the meaning of her name, which in Russian meant friend.

"You are a good storyteller, and you seem to have a good heart," she replied as she picked up her plate and took it to the sink.

"Would it be possible to take a tour of the house?

And may I sit in the living room or maybe at the kitchen table to do some work," Ian asked as she returned trying to give him more food.

"No, thank you," Ian said as he kept her from serving him more.

"Yes, I will show you around. You may use the living room and the kitchen.

However, after nine you must be quiet. This is the time I go to sleep. If you make too much noise, I will let you know," she said as she took the food back to the stove.

"Let's do the tour now and then I will come back and clean the kitchen," she said as she led the way toward the front of the house.

Ian followed her to the entry that opened to the street. This was opposite of the entry leading to the courtyard.

It was quite a large old home, with an entry foyer with a sitting room to one side and a formal dining room on the other. The other entry to the dining room was from the kitchen. Stairs went up from the sitting room side of the foyer.

The master bedroom was over the dining room and there were two more small bedrooms and a bathroom on the second floor.

The next floor up had three small bedrooms and the bathroom Ian had used earlier. The backstairs came up opposite of the bathroom. The stairs then went up to the floor where his room was located.

"Your room is the biggest and has the best view," Raya said as if she had been asked.

"It is a very big house. I noticed there was only one way into the courtyard in back. Is the courtyard yours," Ian asked?

"Yes, long ago there were no other homes around this house. Over the years the owners sold their property. When our family got the property, it was surrounded as it is today and only the passageway out to the street is still ours…mine," Raya said correcting herself.

It was clear to Ian that Raya was still adjusting to the loss of her husband.

Later in evening after Raya was asleep, Ian tested the roof and crossed along the peek to the other building. He located a steel vent pipe on an inward corner of the building and located the fire escape that went down to the street by the entrance walkway.

Ian easily jumped the walkway gap and checked out the other building where he located another fire escape.

He was making sure he had several escape routes just in case he needed them.

The next morning after a sausage and egg breakfast, Ian took his sketchbook and began wandering along the waterfront. He was sketching as he went.

He stopped at each place ordered a coffee and then he showed the proprietor or the person that seemed in charge the six-by-nine-inch drawing advertising Raya's Bed and Breakfast and asked them if he could post it. He was well received in most places and he left a good tip at each.

He slowly made his way up the river all the way to the boat building site he suspected held the missile development effort.

He easily picked up the surveillance cameras following him and noted their locations. It was obviously the place he was looking for since it was the only warehouse along the waterfront with surveillance cameras.

He was glad to have a legitimate reason for walking the area. By lunch time Ian was about a kilometer downriver from the building of interest. He had just put up an advertisement when two muscle men collared him.

"You are not from around here. What are you doing here," the bigger one asked as he held Ian by the arm?

"I am Demyan Kuzmenko, a US citizen. I am on the way to study the wolf population in the Tundra," Ian said as he lightly pushed on the offending arm.

The hand was removed.

"Please show us your passport and do you have papers authorizing you to be here," he asked?

"Yes, but who are you," Ian asked as he looked directly into the eyes of his inquisitor?

Ian wanted the two to see he was not going to be pushed around.

The other guy was just standing by in a more or less relaxed posture, but his hand was near his chest.

"We are FSB," he said with the voice of authority.

"Do you have any papers," Ian said looking him straight in the eyes.

The hand near the arm pit moved into his vest pocket and pulled out a badge.

It was apparent that both men were armed and that they were truly official.

Ian reached into his jacket pocket and pulled out his passport and the papers describing his mission.

"What do you look for when you are studying the wolf," the larger of the two asked after a moment of reading?

"I see if they are surviving, if they have young pups, I count the size of their packs," Ian explained.

"It's a great way to get away from the wife," Ian joked.

That seemed to lighten the moment.

"How long will you be here," the quiet one asked?

"I am waiting for the freight ship I am on to unload and then take on their next load. When they are done, I will move on with them to the Gulf of Ob. The captain estimated unloading and loading would take about four days," Ian replied.

"Why are you putting up signs for Raya's Bed and Breakfast," the smaller of the two asked as he looked at the drawing Ian had just posted.

Ian said he was staying there. He had learned that Raya's husband had died and that she had lost most of her business. This was his good deed to help her.

"This is very generous of you. Let me warn you not to drink at Egor's pub. That is the place they "recruit" river hands on Sunday nights," the smaller quiet one advised.

Ian had been to Egor's pub to put up a sign. Egor had not let him do it. Ian could easily believe Igor would be in that kind of business.

He thanked both of them for their advice.

Ian ordered a beer and went out to a table that looked down the street toward the boat dock. The two FSB agents got into a black car and drove back toward the boat building facility with the cameras.

Ian could not find any surveillance cameras this far away. He was sure the two had come down looking for him after he had been observed by the camera crew.

He was also sure that his passport number would now be getting checked out. He was counting on his team to be good with the paperwork, but he was going to proceed as quickly as possible.

He continued walking and looking for more restaurants and bars.

He approached the boat building facility down a road that came out exactly at the front gate. He found two bar restaurants one block away from the main gate. He visited each and put up the advertisements.

Then he walked one street away as if looking for more restaurants.

Ian walked one block past the end of the facility and turned down toward the river. There were several waterfront businesses as well as bars.

He stopped in a bar with a river front drinking area and ordered a beer. From this vantage point he could study the upriver side of the building housing the missile system.

The downriver side had another boat building facility as a neighbor. Ian had scouted it from the downriver side and found it to be wide open. He would go tonight and approach from that direction to see if there was a way in from there.

He doubted there would be.

A wayward log floating down the river revealed what Ian had feared he would find. The log floated in toward the dock area. It must have triggered a sensor. A spotlight on the roof came on. It revealed a machine gun emplacement on the roof.

The two guards there just monitored the log and watched it bump into the end of the pier and then float on down the river.

The light went back out.

Ian noticed the black car leaving the facility and slowly driving away past him. Ian got the license number and watched it go straight on down the street. He could see the bridge across the river, and he saw the black car drive across. Ian retrieved his hidden duffel and made a call to a phone number that had accompanied his problem-solving orders.

He needed to know where the two guards resided.

Ian walked back to Raya's Bed and Breakfast. His phone rang as he entered the walk to the courtyard. He stopped and listened as the information he needed came through.

"You have already been successful. I have two new guests. Each paid for a week and they plan on staying for several months. Tonight, dinner is free for you," Raya said with new energy in her voice.

"I am glad that I could help," Ian as he received a hug from her.

That evening Ian left by the roof and climbed down the fire escape of the first building.

He went to the waterfront and found a cab to take him across the river to the address he had been given.

Ian took a cab to a nearby address. He paid for the cab and asked him to wait on the main street and gave him money to wait.

The address to the security guards house took him to a small Tudor style home located down a smaller street.

He walked down the street to the address. No dog was present so the doggy treat he had brought along would not be needed. Ian made his way around the house and noted there did not seem to be an alarm system.

He found the door lock easy to pick and thankfully the door hinges were well oiled.

There was just enough light for him to see. He looked for the familiar place to drop the wallet and all the official cards. Sure enough, there on an entrance table was the ID card and a second key card.

Ian pocketed the two and left the same way he had come in. The backdoor locked as easily as he had unlocked it.

Ian picked up his shoes and went to the corner where he slipped them on and walked to the main street where he took the cab back to Egor's pub.

Total elapsed time six minutes and a few seconds.

"Not bad for a novice," Ian thought to himself.

He had picked Egor's place out of spite.

Ian went in and ordered a beer. He then started a raucous fight by declaring one the boatmen a coward and that he had an atrocious smell. Ian tripped the attacking boatman, sent him flying across the table of two men drinking beer with chasers. Once the fight started he faded to the background and left just as the police arrived in force.

He walked to the gate of the shipyard. He had a hooded sweatshirt on. He was sure they would later be able to easily identify him. But for now, he hoped they would be slow in their reaction.

The key card got him in, and he proceeded to look both ways down two crossing hallways. There was a light coming from one of the rooms to his left. He quickly proceeded to the room with the light. He figured it would be the night watch.

Ian looked in and showed the guard facing him the ID card he had in his left hand. He stepped toward the guard and just as he was about to say something, Ian hit him in the side of his head with the heal of his hand. The guard was still standing as Ian made his way past him and caught the second watchman as he turned in his chair.

Both guards were out. Ian taped both guards into their chairs and then taped both of them back-to-back. He finished the job by taping their mouths shut.

He had brought his own supply of duct tape. He hoped to use all of it. The more he used the fewer people would die.

There was a layout of the warehouse on the wall. Ian studied it and found there were three additional night watch offices and the riverside gun tower.

He made his way to each watch office and quickly incapacitated the people that he found there. He felt very good to have taken out the three offices without any real resistance. It was obvious these folks did not expect anyone to try to break in.

Ian approached the roof cautiously. He carefully cracked open the door leading onto the roof. He could see the square platform of the gun tower.

The gun tower guards were sitting looking out toward the river and quietly talking.

The flat roof was a tar and gravel surface. Ian did not want to try to cross to the tower. He was sure he would make too much noise.

He would instead see if he could get the guards to come to him.

Ian coughed and then he let the stairway door go slowly closed.

Both of the guards stood up and walked toward the door. When the first guard opened the stair way door, Ian pulled him all the way in and closed the door. He launched the guard down the stairs.

He then let the door go and pulled in the second guard and hit him in the throat just hard enough for him to momentarily be unable to breath.

Ian went sliding down the metal stair railing and quickly taped the wrists of the recovering guard.

"Relax and breath slowly," he said quietly.

The second guard had recovered and came charging down the stairway as he tried to get his gun free from its strapped down position.

Ian reached up and pulled him toward him and hit him on the back side of the neck. The guard went out cold.

After securely taping the second guards hands behind his back, He pulled both down a well waxed tile hallway to the closest surveillance office.

He made sure everyone was still well secured before making his way to the missile development area.

Ian knew that his action would have little impact on the development of smart missiles. He was sure his mission was more about tweaking the Russian leaders about the vulnerability of one of their most secret projects.

He wiped all the computers memories, their file allocation tables and then magnetized them.

He loaded all the computers, and all the records he could find, the missiles and their guidance system into one of the river boat hulls.

He then filled the hull with a supply of dry lumber and doused everything with gasoline. He launched the boat with a cloth napkin burning on a piece of dry lumber with its tail in a puddle of gas.

Ian figured he had about ten minutes before there was a huge fire ball floating down the river. Ian pulled all the guards into the hallway leading to the front door. He then used the can of gasoline he had found in the development area and poured a stream along all the hallways and the watch rooms.

He was ready to finish the job. He pulled all the guards outside and across the empty street. He then threw a burning wad of paper into the building.

Ian walked up away from the river as the place went up in flames. It lit up the entire neighborhood. At almost the same time the boat on the river burst into flames. It was a grand scene. The missiles exploded in a climactic scene that mirrored a fourth of July river barge fire and explosion of all the fireworks on the Ohio River that Ian had witnessed.

He returned to the building he had climbed down by Raya's B&B. He climbed back up and went into his room.

He was not staying.

The entire neighborhood was now up and going toward the fire.

He gathered his things. He took the drawings of Raya and penned a note thanking her for a good stay and put it on the kitchen table with a significant tip.

He went back up to his room and left by the window. He went to the other building.

The FSB guys must have done their homework. Ian caught a glimpse of them coming up the narrow walkway toward Raya's B&B.

He went to the drainpipe at the corner of the building and slid down. He walked by the end of the entrance walkway. The black car was sitting at the corner. It had the keys in it. He got in and drove away. He saw the two come out to the street. He drove across the bridge and headed toward Syerdlovsk. He hoped the two would not have the police chase him.

"There goes our car. Should I call the police for help," the larger of the two asked?

"Are you kidding, he would end up killing them. He was in my house and took my security card. I thought he seemed very sure of himself when we confronted him. I wonder who he is?

He could have killed all the guards, but he made sure they were all safe before setting the fire. I really hope he gets out, so we don't have to answer any questions about why we didn't bring him in when we first stopped him and why he was able to take our car," the quiet one replied.

Ian drove carefully and was pleased that there was no pursuit. He reached the train station area of Syerdlovsk.

He found an old, abandoned house and drove the car into the garage. He caught a cab to the train station, got his bag, changed into his business suit, and took the train back to T'bilisi.

Two days later he flew from T'bilisi to Frankfurt and caught a flight to California.

He was looking forward to getting home, so he caught a red eye special to Cincinnati and arrived early on a Saturday.

Lesley had the coffee brewing and after a hug she fixed breakfast. Ella was still sleeping.

Ian gave Lesley a kiss and thanked her for a great breakfast.

Lesley sat down and said she had two surprise announcements.

The first was that she knew of a home that was part of a divorce agreement. It was up for sale at a bargain price. She had gone and taken tour and said it would be perfect for them.

Ian of course agreed to go look at it when she asked if he would go with her later in the day.

The second announcement was that she was pregnant.

Ian sat and let the news soak slowly through.

Lesley was expecting more excitement and asked if he was OK with that.

He stood up and pulled her to him and gave her a hug and a kiss.

Of course, he was. He was slowly covering the black space in his mind with more glowing warm blankets.

62

Chapter 4: Border Crosser – The Devil, the Drivers

Ian took the same route back as the one he had taken out from Phoenix. The white panel truck was gone. He had expected it to be.

As the miles clicked over, Ian was more certain of a high probability that there was a connection in one of the law enforcement agencies. He pondered how he might determine who that person might be.

He came to the conclusion that there needed to be a connection or helper in the border patrol organization. He was more confident in finding that person. His focus area was on the drone monitoring team. He thought that person might need help to coordinate their actions.

Ian arrived at the federal building and parked his car in the basement next to all the other non-descript government vehicles.

He decided first to find out what had happened to the group of people he had help and then were caught at Interstate 40.

The sergeant on duty at the highway patrol desk looked at his computer screen and let him know that they had been sent to homeland security for the normal entrance processing. Each would have their day in court.

The sergeant went on to let Ian know that two of the people picked up were still in the holding cell. They had been picked up walking in their briefs and no shoes. They had admitted to driving the panel truck that had hauled the border crossers away from the border. They wanted a lawyer and were threatening to sue because they claimed some policeman beat them up. They were in a sorry state and their feet were bleeding when they were picked up.

They were to be transferred to the city jail because the city had jurisdiction since the two lived here in Phoenix. The police would be picking them up sometime in the afternoon.

Ian asked the sergeant not to let the transfer happen until he heard from captain Martin.

He let the sergeant know that he planned to return immediately afterwards to talk with the two being held.

The sergeant told him good luck on getting them to talk. They have refused until they get a lawyer.

Ian had doubted the two in the holding cell about some high-ranking official in the highway patrol being the leader. When Ian learned of the transfer to the city police a red flag went up.

The two had survived the night in highway patrol custody. He immediately transferred his suspicion to the city police.

He went to May's to get some ammunition.

He approached Mathew's support, Marilyn, with her favorite cup of latte from May's and handed it to her as he walked past her and told her he had to talk to the boss.

She informed him that she was supposed to stop him but made no move to do so but instead took a sip of her latte and raised one eyebrow and said thanks.

Ian handed an angry looking Matt a plain cup of May's coffee as Matt excused himself on the phone and hung up.

What the hell, I told Marilyn to keep everyone out. Then he stopped.

"Thanks, I suppose you bribed your way in with a latte for Marilyn. What's up?" Mathew said as he took his coffee. He was surprised that he was getting to like Herman.

Ian apologized for his disruption but came right to the point that someone in the Phoenix police department was involved in managing the transport of border crossers.

He went on to explain that the Highway Patrol had the two drivers of the transport in a holding cell. They were scheduled to be picked up by someone from the police department in the afternoon.

Ian then put forward the theory that the two would never reach the city jail alive but would be killed during their escape attempt.

Matt made the comment that he had just started to like him.

He wanted to know how Ian could possibly have gotten such information since his department had tried to question the two and had gotten nothing from them.

He went on to say that Ian did not seem to be such a trusting person that the two would just volunteer the information to him.

Ian gave a small laugh. He shared the fact that he had locked the two up in the back of the panel truck and threatened to keep them there until they cooked to death. It was hot enough that they gave him just enough information. I released them.

Your men picked them up along the road soon after. You saw and treated their condition. That was also my doing.

Matt simply said Oh! That explains their police brutality claim.

"So how do you figure it is somebody high up in the Phoenix police department and not someone in the Highway Patrol. Why not me," Matt inquired?

"Well, the two in the holding cell informed me that someone, high up in the Highway Patrol department had hired them. Since they are still alive today, I figured it wasn't you or anyone in your organization," Ian said with a smile.

Ian pointed out that the two really had no clue as to the actual person or persons might be. They got their orders and their pay via the internet. They could easily have been misdirected on purpose.

"What kind of help are you asking for," Mathew inquired?

"I want the two men to wear a wire and I want your department to follow the city police transport and listen in to the situation,"

Matt first defended, Bill, the chief of police. There is no way he would be involved and do such a thing. He does not need money and has grandchildren that he spends all his free time with. Matt said he thought that the idea was crazy.

Ian replied that he did not think it was Bill but asked that he be kept out of the loop in the near term. He was sure that the culprit had to be someone Bill trusted. Ian pointed out that they would know almost immediately if there was someone in the sheriff's office and at breakfast tomorrow Ian would personally apologize to Bill if he was wrong.

Matt said he would support Ian, but he did not think that the two in custody would agree to wear a wire. If they did wear a wire and made it safely to the city jail, he would have hell to pay with Bill.

Ian agreed and again said he would put himself in front of that train if he was wrong. He said he would not have asked if he did not believe he was right.

Matt was under the impression that the two would not agree to wear a wire. They have been stonewalling ever since they arrived, they wanted a lawyer.

Ian replied that he would convince them to wear a wire. And asked that Matt call Mike and have him come over.

Ian walked back downstairs to the desk sergeant. He asked to be taken to the holding cell.

The desk sergeant stopped in amazement as the two inside the cell jumped up and stood up at attention. He looked at Ian and commented that there was something about Ian that these two respected. The two had so far refused to stand because the condition of their feet.

Ian approached the cell and simply said hello. He asked about their claim that they had been mistreated. He asked if there was some complaint, they would like to share with him?

They both shook their head to indicate no. The strained look on their faces almost made Ian laugh.

The sergeant commented that the two had been a pain when the highway patrol tried to question them. They had refused to even talk. You say hello and they immediately stand at attention.

Ian had made a point of learning the sergeant's name. He now let Bob know that he needed a few moments alone with the two. He asked for about ten minutes. After that have the folks who will outfit the two with wires come in to do so.

Bob commented that it was a little unusual but said that if Ian needed anything he should just press the buzzer on the wall.

Ian told the two in the cell to sit down and listen. He asked them if they knew they were being transferred to the city jail. They said they had been told that.

Ian asked if they believed they would live to see the inside of the sheriff's jail cell.

Eduardo, the tall one, asked who Ian was. Manuel the shorter one reminded him that than Ian claimed to be the devil.

Ian replied that he certainly was willing to play the part of the devil but in their case, he was trying to save their lives. He pointed out that he was interested in the person or persons at the top of the ladder that paid them.

He told them they would be dead by late this afternoon if they did not cooperate. Whoever the people in the police department may be, they will kill you as you try to escape.

Eduardo asked why they would try to escape. They had received good treatment so far.

Ian told them they would be taken somewhere at the edge of the city and told to go home. After they stepped out of the police van, they would be shot in the back with the cover story that they were trying to escape.

Ian let the silence stand. Then he stood and reached for the buzzer and he told them good luck getting to heaven.

Manuel asked what they needed to do?

Ian informed them that they needed to wear a hidden microphone so he could hear what the men picking them up were saying. He said he expected those transporting them would probably be friendly and tell the two that they were going to be dropped off outside the city limits. You will be instructed to go home, get your stuff and to move on. They will tell you they will send instructions to you later. Or they will tell you some other similar story. However, when they let you out of the police van, they will shout out "stop" and as either you run or turn around to look at them, they will shoot you.

How do you know this Eduardo asked?

Ian replied he would do something similar if he were the person in the police department managing the operation.

Eduardo then said they would cooperate. He wanted to know how Ian would help them afterwards.

Ian replied that they would be held accountable for their deeds and they faced up to thirty years in jail, however he would make sure they got the best possible deal for their cooperation and would probably only get a fraction of that time.

Eduardo looked at Manuel. The two were silent for a moment and then agreed to wear the wire.

Ian gave a nod and let them know that they would soon be outfitted with the microphones.

Ian went to the sergeant and asked where he would take the two if he was planning to kill them and make it look like and escape.

The sergeant gave a good chuckle and smiled. He went on to explain that the scenario that Ian had just described was the talk of almost every beer drinking outing that the local law enforcement held.

One group had the scenario playing out somewhere south of East Dobbins Road out on South Central Avenue. Another group talks about going out on the 303 or the 74 west of I 17. A third group talks about going out on 87 north. It's all just talk.

The sergeant went on to comment that almost any short drive outside the city would do. There were many secluded out of the way places.

The sergeant asked if he had passed the test.

Ian pointed out that looking at the city map he figured the police van should go southeast down North West Grand Avenue. Ian was trying to figure out where it was most likely to go if the police van deviated from that route.

The sergeant put his finger on the map and said he would take them out on that road.

Ian asked the sergeant to make sure that the drivers of the city police van did not know what was going down.

He was pleased to hear the sergeant exclaim that if there were any crooked cops in Phoenix, he wanted them caught and punished.

Chapter 5: Border Crosser – A Short Ride

Ian walked slowly up the stairs. He could hear the coon dogs yelping as they got the scent of their prey. He could see the stars overhead as his gas head lantern lit the way before him. He could feel the adrenaline rush. He was closing in for the kill. His adrenalin level was at its peak.

Ian knew that it was only a matter of time. He realized he did not know how many people worked for Mike. By now Mike should be in Matt's office. Matt had mentioned he would have his team ready to go. Ian needed at least four different cars to follow the police van. He did not want the driver to notice he was being followed.

Matt was sitting with Mike discussing the logistics of moving the various cars along the direction the city police transport van would take. Mike was in control of four cars and the chief said he had as many.

Ian asked Matt to be in charge of positioning the eight vehicles and that he would just be along for the ride. He also requested that the people in all the vehicles be in street clothes.

Matt gave a small laugh. He said the sergeant downstairs figures you are the one in charge of everything that is going down and he said to help or get out of the way.

Ian looked at Matt and Mike. He could see that they too had the adrenaline rush going. He suggested a quick lunch would help all of them.

During lunch Ian kept the conversation on family and events going on in the city. He wanted to keep the focus away from the coming action.

At three the pickup occurred. The dark blue van with Phoenix City Police painted on the sides pulled into the State Trooper's pick-up area. The shackled, Edwardo and Manuel were led out and put into the back of the van. As per protocol seat belts were put on before the doors were closed.

Ian watched as the van went in the right direction down North West Grand Avenue. It was headed in the right direction. He wondered if he was wrong.

A few moments later a call came in letting them know that the van had turned off Grand Avenue and was headed south down 19th Avenue.

Ian was listening in on the conversation that was going on in the city police transport van. The conversation with Edwardo and Manuel was almost verbatim to what Ian had told them they would hear.

He was sure the two were now paying very close attention to what was going on.

The transport turned east on West Dobbins. It appeared that Ian would be buying Bob, the sergeant at the desk a beer. Bob had said that the southern scenario would be the one he would choose.

Ian listened as Matt instructed three of the cars to head south on South Central. He positioned two cars north of the intersection.

The cars tailing the van kept switching so that they would not be discovered.

Matt and Ian were following behind all of them as Matt directed the flow of the cars like a chess master playing in a tournament.

The van made the expected right turn and headed south on South Central avenue.

Matt instructed the three lead cars to go just past where South-Central crossed Phoenix South Mountain Park. He was counting on the fact that the park provided the right conditions for the planned killing.

Matt had all the cars closing in from behind. His car was up front.

Ian continued listening to what was going on in the van. The van drove into a secluded area at the entrance to the park.

The tailing highway patrol vehicles parked, and everyone ran out to surround the city police van. It seemed to him they were generating a hell of a racket. Ian was surprised they had not been discovered.

Ian was standing by a tree directly behind the van. He did not need his headset to hear Eduardo and Manuel being told to get out and find their way home.

Ian heard the escape call going into the city police dispatch office. The two transport policemen were just raising their guns to fire when he stepped out and shouted for them to put their guns down. They were surround and they were under arrest.

The two foolishly turned and fired at him. He took one bullet in the chest, but the other shot missed. He knelt and returned fire. He shot each of them in the leg. He was sure they were wearing bullet proof vests like himself, so he shot both of them in the chest. He wanted them alive.

Matt and Mike rushed over to Ian. They were amazed that the forty-five-slug embedded in the vest had not knocked Ian down.

They were more amazed that Ian had taken down the other two in such a fashion that they would live to be prosecuted.

Ian knew he would have a large chest bruise accompanied by an ache once the adrenalin rush subsided.

Mike took over the scene. An ambulance was on the way to take the two wounded policemen to the hospital. He assigned two of his agents to stand guard over the two policemen going to the hospital.
They were instructed to only let himself, Matt, or Ian in.

Ian asked to have a word alone with the two he had shot.

Ian walked over to the two who were still laying on the ground. He let them know that he knew they had help back in the city police department. They needed to make a choice to save their skin or get the maximum time of around thirty years for shooting an FBI agent and they would get the maximum time for being accessories to the death of thirty people in the back of the van discovered a few weeks ago.

Ian waited for a count of thirty. OK, keep quiet, it's your funeral. I am sure those above you will make sure you never get to talk. They will transfer your money in the offshore bank accounts to their own and freeze you out. Then they will make sure you never get to trial.

Ian watched the surprised look on their faces. It had just occurred to them that they might be killed.

Ian was standing to leave when he was asked about the deal. They would give him information for a good deal.

Ian got back down on one knee. He told them it would be a deal that kept them alive, off death row and perhaps assignment to a low security prison. He told them they would go to jail and would serve some significant time.

The two looked at each other then asked what Ian wanted to know.

Ian told them he wanted the name of the top guy.

They both whispered the name Bradley Peterson.

Ian said thank you and stood up. He looked over at one of the agents and told him to read them their rights and stay with them in the ambulances. Guard them well and keep them alive and arrange lawyers for them.

One of the highway patrol officers asked what to do with Eduardo and Manuel.

Matt responded that the two should be taken back to the station and put back into the holding cell. He would deal with them at a later time.

Matt, and Mike approached Ian. They wanted to know the name that the two policemen had given him.

Ian watched Matt as he gave out the name of Bradley Peterson.

Matt was surprised and said so. He commented that Bradley was second in command and that he was considered next in line to take over the sheriff's office.

Matt said he would give Bill a call and tell him to isolate Bradley and not let him destroy any records. Damn this is not going to be pretty Matt continued.

Ian was ready for the killing blow.

He suggested they all go to Bill's office and confront Bradley together. Ian made a call to his help number and requested a quick rundown on the finances of Bradley Peterson.

As the three arrived at the city police station, Ian received a call back on the finances for Bradley. Bradley was living very well for someone making one hundred thousand dollars a year. So far there seemed to be no indication of anything unusual in his bank accounts. They were not sure where he had gotten the money for a very high-level living style.

Ian told the group to check for transactions with any offshore account.

Bradley was sitting in Bob's office when the three walked in. Bob immediately commented that the request he had fulfilled was very unusual and he hoped there was a very good reason.

Ian looked at Bradley and formally put him under arrest for conspiracy against the US government. Ian was acting as if the case was clear and complete. He went on to list the fact that Bradley had aided and abetted the crossing of thousands of illegal aliens. It was most likely that he would be indicted for the deaths of more than thirty people found in the back of a panel truck perhaps both trucks. He informed Bradley that he had been identified by two of his participating members who had turned state's evidence.

He asked Bradley what he had to say?

Bradley replied that the charges were preposterous. He refused to say anything until his lawyer was present.

That's fine the FBI is already in the process of confiscating your computer and all you records, your secretary's computer and records, your associates computer, and records. They have also entered your home and secured your home computer and any records you had there.

The FBI has also moved to freeze all your offshore accounts.

Your cooperation would be useful, but I prefer you refuse so that you get the death penalty, Ian continued as he leaned in almost nose to nose to Bradley.

Ian did not have most of the information he had said he had but he was in the mood to play poker and go for the winning hand via a bluff.

Bradley stood up and said he would consult with his lawyer and got up to leave.

Ian blocked his way and asked whether he had not understood that he was under arrest and that his lawyer would need to come to him. Meanwhile he would cool his heals behind bars.

Ian turned to two police officers standing in the room and told them to handcuff Bradley and read him his rights. The two looked at each other and finally one of them took his handcuffs and put them on. The other read Bradly his Miranda rights.

Ian turned to Bill and asked him if any of his officers had left early today. It will probably be one of the guys working in dispatch. Ian went on to conjecture that there would be four or five individuals involved.

Ian's phone rang, and he held up his hand to stop the two police officers that were escorting Bradley out.

He went into an excited conversation and commented how much easier it was going to be to wrap up the investigation. He went on to thank the person on the line for making the connection to the offshore accounts happen so quickly. Ian instructed the person online to contact Mike Lancaster in the Phoenix office as soon as the bank accounts were secured.

Everyone in the room heard Ian's end of the conversation. The person on the other end wondered what was going on. He had been ready to tell Ian that it would take a while to identify and track down the offshore accounts.

Ian went on to comment how much easier it was going to be having made the link to the offshore accounts. Looking directly at Bradley he commented that it would have been smarter to use different offshore banks.

Ian walked over to Bradley and put his lips close to his ear and whispered, "if you don't talk, you won't live to see morning. I am an assassin sent to eliminate any obstacle to the resolution to this problem. If you talk you live."

Ian then pulled away only far enough to stare directly into Bradley's eyes. Then he turned and sat on the edge of Bob's desk.

Ian asked Bradley if he had anything to say?

"Alright, I am involved but Sam Henderson has been the mastermind of the operation. I provided a shield for the operation," Bradley confessed.

Ian was pleased with Bradley's reaction. Ian's threat had been real.

Ian turned to Mike and asked him to have a couple of his agents document Bradley's confession. They were to take down everything he knew about the operation and its finances. Have the remainder of those involved in the operation picked up.

Mike commented that the offshore bank link had really been found very fast. He had never heard of being able to track money so fast.

Once Bradley was out of the room, Ian let everyone know that the call had been to inform him that it would take a couple of days to a few weeks to track the accounts and that it would probably be impossible to tell where in the US the funds were coming from or going to. They needed more information from this end.

Everyone in the room agreed with Mike that it was one hell of a bluff. They all agreed that Ian was barred from their Saturday poker games.

Ian let that stand. He knew that it was his death threat that had tipped the scale.

He looked around and commented that they were almost done. When asked what remained, Ian pointed out that someone in Homeland Security had to be involved. The successes of the crossings were not an accident. The person or persons involved were as guilty of deaths of two truckloads of people as the driver and those arranging the border crossings.

Chapter 6: Border Crosser – Drone Operator

It all started one evening as he sat watching the Arizona Diamondbacks at the sports bar. Trey was approached by a man that introduced himself as Sam. Sam had done his homework and knew Trey was sympathetic to the plight of the border crossers. He proposed a working relationship that offered a little extra money and a lot of personal satisfaction of helping people get to their dream. All he had to do was to misdirect the border patrol he was guiding. It would only take a few minutes, and no one would ever know.

The statement, "no one would ever know" alarmed Trey. How did Sam know so much about him? Trey replied that he would think about it.

A few weeks went by and Trey had almost forgotten about the offer. Then he was on duty as a group of crossers refused to stop when confronted by the border guards. They scattered and began to run and one of the guards pull out his gun and began to fire. Two to the crossers were hit. One was just wounded in the leg but a young boy in his early teens died on the scene.

Trey had watched the entire confrontation from his drone camera.

That incident made up his mind that he wanted to help the border crossers.

That weekend Sam again made contact with him at the sports bar.

Since that time, Trey had been aiding in the crossings by miss-positioning the guards.

Then he saw the news report about the dead border crossers piled in the back of a panel truck. He vowed he would not misdirect the border guards again. He knew that most border crossers were trying for a better life in the US would be sent back. Those who truly were seeking asylum in fear of their lives would be processed and get their day in court.

He had played god and at least fifty people were dead.

He was not in it for the money and did not even bring money up when he was recruited. When finally asked about money, he inquired about the amount. It was to be two thousand a month. Trey agreed that is was significant, but he personally did not need or want it.

Trey pushed a piece of paper across the table to Sam. There were three organizations on it: Red Cross Relief Fund, United Appeal, Catholic Social Services. He bargained for more by asking that each organization get seven hundred dollars each month and that a confirmation post card be sent to him.

Sam readily agreed to the arrangement. He would have paid double that amount if asked.

The redirecting went on smoothly until the abandoned truck with all the bodies had made the news. Matt was shocked and wondered if he had contributed to the deaths of the people. In his mind he was sure that he had.

Two trucks abandoned in the middle of the desert. The sun making the metal skin of the panel truck's metal exterior hot enough to fry an egg. People abandoned to die in the suffocating oven like heat. Humans so desperate that they broke their bodies against the backdoors in an attempt to break out. Humans so desperate that their fingernails ripped out in their attempt to claw their way out.

These were constant elements of Trey's nightmares. But the scene of the two dead children being lovingly held to their mother's dead chest played in both his sleep and daylight cycles. He could not shake the vision and the knowledge that he was part of putting those people through the hell of their last few hours of their lives.

Trey knew he was on the verge of a mental breakdown. He loathed himself. He had succumbed to the lure of easy money for helping those poor border crossers. He truly was sympathetic to their cause. He now believed he had made a deal with the devil. He had sold his soul for a small bag of gold.

He went to the bar several times hoping to make contact with Sam. But it never happened.

The reality of his situation hit Trey hard. He took vacation and drank himself into a stupor for two weeks.

He vowed he would not misdirect the border guards again.

He had played god and at least fifty people were dead.

Trey returned to work and followed his conscious for the following week. Then the signal for misdirection came into him.

He ignored it and the group coming across was apprehended.

He got a call at his home that night. He was told that if he missed the next misdirection signal, he would lose the sight of his left eye and the loss of one finger. If he did as he was told, he would get a ten percent bonus for each event.

Trey immediately understood that he was indeed working for the devil and he was in a trap. He would suffer dearly for not following orders.

He wrote down the phone number from which the threat had been made. He did not know how to trace it to a source but a friend of his probably could.

Trey imagined finding the culprit and taking some sort of action to protect himself.

He realized immediately that he did not have the courage to follow through. He knew he was being threatened by one of the cartels in Mexico.

He could accept them killing him. He deserved being killed. He could not imagine or accept the torture they were threatening.

Two days later he again got the signal to misdirect a specific border security team.

Trey diverted the border guards just to the west of where the crossing was to occur. The truck was parked only a mile from the boarder in a small ravine. It was visible from the air but the team on the ground did not see it as they passed only a few hundred yards away.

Trey complied but it came to him that someone else was also on the take. Each time the misdirection was targeted at a specific team and at a specific time. He had never thought about this key fact. Someone else in the organization who knew the schedule and location of the security teams had to be involved.

Trey began keeping track of which schedulers were on duty on the days he got the misdirection signal.

Again, Trey came to the realization that when he figured out who it was, he was not sure what he would do.

He wondered if he could leave the region and not be found.

A few days later the FBI toured the drone control facility. Trey listened as the supervisor explained the interaction of the drone operators with the various border patrol teams.

He figured his days were numbered. It was clear to him that the older FBI agent was in charge. He listened intently and asked the kind of questions that made it clear he understood how easily it would be for a drone operator to misdirect the action on the ground.

Trey thought about the old saying about being between a rock and a hard place. He figured he was between hell and if extremely lucky a long term in jail if he could avoid a death sentence.

At this point jail seemed to be the safest place to be. Trey thought about his complicity and the thought of a death sentence silenced him.

Trey succumbed to drinking himself asleep each night. He awakened in the morning to his nightmares. His work life was miserable. He barely ate. He was a mess.

Trey knew that the noose around his neck was tightening. He did not know how much longer he could take his self-inflicted pressure.

He made a point of documenting everything he knew about the situation.

He had made up his mind. He was going to take his own life. It was the only pain free way to escape the situation he was in.

He wondered if his parents would understand. He was their only child. He took the time to write them a letter explaining his situation and said he loved them and hoped they would forgive him.

All that remained was to work up the courage to do it and he knew that deep inside he was a coward.

He was at work and in the process of again misdirecting a field team of border guards when he again observed the FBI agent come into the Border Security office.

Trey immediately knew what he was going to do.

First, he walked over to the shredder and put in the suicide letter to his parents.

Chapter 7: Closure

The several hour ride to the Homeland Security offices provided Mike and Ian time to talk.

Mike asked what Ian had whispered to Bradley to get him to confess so fast.

Ian shared that he had reminded Bradley that it was going to be a long night and he was not going to have to give up his belt or tie, but much could happen to him before the sun came up. Bradley's imagination did the rest. Ian left out the part where he told Bradley he was the assassin sent out to kill whoever was behind the truck incident.

The drive through the bleak desert terrain of patches of tumble weeds, cactuses and some dry looking grasses seemed to compliment the stones, blowing dirt or maybe brown sand and a wide dead looking terrain. The sky was cloudless. Ian figured it was too hot for any moisture to rise and condense. He wondered when the last rain had been.

He was glad to let Mike do the driving since it gave him time reflect.

He relaxed and concentrated on how they would flush out the guilty party or parties at the Homeland office. Ian suspected that there was more than one person involved. He expected at least one person to be a drone operator. Such a person would be able to misguide the group personnel, so the border crossers could pass by, but timing was a key factor.

They were to again meet with Tom Hemsley, the station supervisor. Ian hoped Tom was not involved. It would really be a bad situation if he were.

Tom was standing by to receive the FBI agents coming to meet with him. He had worked with Mike over the last several years and had attended a cookout where his family and Matt's family had shared a picnic table. They both had kids of about the same age. His kids were asking when there was going to be another police picnic in Phoenix.

On the other hand, the FBI agent that was currently helping Matt scared the bejesus out of him. His penetrating gaze and his direct and rather aggressive manner made Tom nervous. He knew it would not be a good idea to get in his way.

Tom had one of his crew out scouting for an incoming car. He did not want any surprises. He would meet the two in the parking lot before bringing them into the building. Once they entered everyone in the building would know and wonder why the two had come back again.

Ian saw the Homeland Security agent riding an RTV alongside of the highway. He figured him for a scout out verifying the incoming traffic.

Ian let Mike know that Tom knew that they were arriving. And it appeared that he was nervous about their arrival. Ian conjectured that perhaps they should have told him more about their purpose in coming. It would have been easier if they could totally count him and his immediate reports out. But Ian questioned what would have happened in their interactions at the sheriff's office if Bob had shared any information with Bradley.

Mike looked at Ian and decided never to play poker or chess with him. He knew Ian would not cheat. He would just figure out how to beat you. It was clear to Mike that Herman Lunquist never left anything to chance.

Mike agreed with Ian. His personal connection with Tom and his family gave him confidence that Tom was in the clear.

He did not know how but he was confident that Herman would find the guilty.

Ian saw Tom standing under the building entrance canopy on the edge of the parking lot. Tom pointed to an empty parking space almost directly in front of the canopy. Matt parked in the space to which Tom pointed.

Tom greeted Matt with a handshake and a man hug. Ian liked him for doing that. Ian was a hugger with people he knew.

Tom gave Ian a formal and firm handshake.

Before escorting them in, Tom wanted to know why the FBI was back and in such a cryptic fashion.

It took all his inner strength and control, but he glanced at Mike and then focused on Ian.

Ian smiled. Tom's actions made it clear to Ian that Tom stood by his people. He was a protector. He would be devastated if one of his were involved in helping the smugglers, smuggle people across the border that he was sworn to patrol and enforce. This was going to be as hard on him as it had been on the sheriff.

Ian quietly told Tom that one or more of his people were corrupt. He had come to determine who in the drone team was involved and who on the scheduling team was involved. Ian figured that the two positions would be minimum number involved in the border crossing scheme.

He asked Tom if that was a problem?

Tom got angry and asked how the hell Ian was so sure one of his people were involved.

Ian calmly replied that it was more than one and that it was the only explanation that fit the situation.

Mike decided to break the tension. He explained what had just transpired in Phoenix where the second in command of the police department had confessed to hiring the truck drivers and having the trucks rented.

Tom stood silently for a moment. Then he muttered, "Jesus this is going to play hell with our organization if some of our folks are involved. They are likely to get shot by their angry coworkers."

Ian pointed out that it was time for them to go in and figure out how to spot the perpetrators.

Tom nodded and led the way into the building and up to his office.

From his window desk on the second floor Trey saw the trio walking in. He knew the jig was up. He was glad. He walked over to the shredder and shredded the suicide letter he had delayed sending to his parents.

He was going to turn himself in. He would not wait to be interrogated. He wasn't sure what the penalty was for what he had done but it couldn't be worse than the sleepless nights and continuous anguish that he was now experiencing. He figured it was one step above suicide.

He got up, walked to Tom's office where the three were meeting and knocked on the door.

Ian was surprised as Trey walked in and simply said that he was the one they were looking for. Someone turning themselves in had not been on Ian's list of how to find the perpetrator.

Ian stood up and asked Trey to take his seat. He also wanted to see Tom's reaction.

Ian asked Trey to explain why the FBI would be interested in him.

Trey held up a thumb drive and explained that he had documented all he knew about how the border crossings were managed. He explained that he periodically received a divert signal and the time and place of the diversion of the ground guard team to be diverted. Trey commented on the fact that he had come to the conclusion one of the schedulers had to be involved.

Ian asked how long Trey had been doing this and how he had been recruited.

Trey said it is all detailed on this thumb drive.

Ian thanked Trey for the documentation but said he wanted to hear it in Trey's own word. He asked Tom to record Trey's confession. He asked Mike to read Trey his Miranda rights. He took the thumb drive and gave it to Mike.

Trey had tears in his eyes. It was hard for him to see. The flood of emotion was overwhelming him.

He began to cry.

Through his crying he explained that the vision of the dead mother holding her two dead children to her chest would be with him forever. If there was a hell, he said he was sure to go there. He was sure that truck had been one of the ones used when he had diverted the ground crew.

Ian looked at Tom and asked if there was a secure room where Trey could be put.

Ian wanted time to review what was on the thumb drive, so they could determine their next steps.

Ian asked that Tom, Mike, and he together review the contents of the thumb drive.

After locking Trey in a secure room, Tom plugged the thumb drive into his computer and opened the only file that was on it.

It was clear that Trey had provided a detailed account of his recruitment. He had provided the time and dates of all the diversions. Trey had come to the realization that a person in scheduling had to also be involved and had narrowed it down to two people.

Ian scanned all the information. He came to a much more startling theory.

Trey had not done it for the money, but the scheduler most probably had done it for money. The cartels had billions of dollars with which to work. Sam, or whatever his real name, most probably recruited multiple people. Why stop at one. There was money to be made. He would want to have backups. He would recruit as many people as possible.

He looked at Tom and could see that he was angry about what was transpiring. Ian knew that if he were in Tom's position, he would be wondering who else was on the take. This was probably Tom's most dreaded situation.

Tom personally knew one of the two, Maurice, as a true family man and an upstanding member of his church. He picked Tim as the most likely one to be recruited. He was the one that was forever coming up with an excuse for being late to work and he dressed in slovenly manner.

The selection made little sense to Ian. He had known too many family men who had let their ego and desire for personal goods sell out their families.

Ian walked out of the office and put in a call to his support team. He asked them to check out the two schedulers. He asked that they especially look at the bank accounts and spending habit change. They were also to look through the background clearance checks and see if there were any gaps in the information.

He returned and asked Tom to bring in the person he suspected.

A young looking, man that probably got carded every time he ordered a drink came through the door. Ian stepped forward and shook hands with Tim. Tim appeared to be sixteen but was probably in his early thirties. He sported a scraggly beard and a head of hair that was greased and made into spikes. What Ian took to be a punk head.

It was clear that Tom did not especially like Tim and that Tim knew this and probably presented himself in the way he did as a way to irritate Tom.

Almost instantly Ian figured it was the family man that would be the culprit. Tim seemed too confident and together to be the one.

Ian also concluded that Tom was a biased judge of character.

Mike watched Ian's interactions with Tim. Ian pressed him on how he scheduled his teams. He pressed Tim hard about the timing and placement of the teams and who he shared this information with.

Ian then probed into Tim's personal life. Was he single? Yes, did he have a girlfriend? How often did he go out? Where did they go out? Was he getting laid?

Tim remained cool and collected. He calmly answered Ian's questions and even joked with Ian about his poor love life and the fact that there was no place to go in this forsaken part of the world. He did not seem disturbed. He laughed at the last question and answered, "not enough."

Ian thanked Tim for answering his questions and made a point that there would be a follow up the following day.

As Tim was leaving, he invited Ian for a drink if he was staying in town that evening.

Ian turned to Tom and asked him to bring in Maurice for his interview.

Mike came to the conclusion that Maurice was in for a really thorough grilling. It was clear to him that Tim had passed, the grilling he had undergone, with flying colors.

Maurice reminded Mike of Bradley. He was confident that he was above suspicion.

Ian asked similar questions to what he had asked Tim. The answers Maurice gave were always logical and often supported with examples of his family and church life.

Ian decided it was time to use the one threat that he knew would work.

Ian leaned in close to Maurice's ear. He whispered a curse, "you god damn soulless son of a bitch. I have your offshore bank account number and the times you refilled your PNC account. I know exactly when you were recruited. I am not an FBI agent. The government does not desire to be embarrassed and has sent me out to eliminate anyone who does not confess to their deeds. You have to the count of twenty and then I leave and tonight you die."

Tom was looking at Mike. He mouthed, "What is he saying?"

Mike just shrugged and tilted his head. He had the gist but had no clue as to the actual words. He watched as Maurice's face went white. To Mike this was the face of someone who was guilty.

Ian stepped back. Maurice put his elbows on his knees and leaned his face into his cupped hands. It was clear that he was crying.

Ian counted slowly to twenty. When he said twenty out loud, Maurice fell to his knees and cried out, "Please forgive me. I just wanted to be a better provider for my family."

Tom looked at Ian with newfound respect. He told Maurice it was not their role to forgive. He would be tried for his misdeeds. A judge and jury would decide his fate.

Ian asked Mike to read Maurice his rights. He looked at Tom who was looking a little pale and appeared to be in a state of shock.

Ian knew that if Tom was kept employed, he was now in line for reassignment to the most remote location possible.

Ian asked that Trey and Maurice be held in custody. He and Matt would transport both Maurice and Trey to Phoenix where they would be arraigned.

Ian knew the follow up investigations would go on for a long time. He looked at Mike and commented that he would have his hands full for the foreseeable future. He was sure that his promotion would help.

The drive to Phoenix was eerily quiet. Ian was sitting in the backseat with Maurice who had his handcuffed hands on his lap.

Trey sat quietly in the right front seat looking out the window. It was clear that he had found whatever peace he would have for the rest of his life. He seemed at calm. Ian figured confession had freed his soul.

Maurice on the other hand went from whimpering to full sobs. He was still wrestling with his demons. Ian would make sure he was put on suicide watch.

The expanse of the desert seemed to go on forever until it met the black and dark green of the Rockies. The blue of the cloudless sky seemed appealing until the heat of the day hit your face.

Ian decided the best thing for him to do was to doze lightly. Mike seemed to be fully concentrating on his driving.

Mike had called ahead and made arrangements with Bill to have space available for the two they were bringing in. He also let him know that each had obtained the services of a lawyer. The lawyers were going to meet their clients the next day. The two would be arraigned on Friday.

Mike planned to hold a news conference in the morning. He asked Ian to take the lead.

Ian declined. He led Mike to believe that it would ruin his future in solving cases like the one they had just solved together.

Mike found this a little hard to believe but he knew the news conference to share the success would certainly help his career. He remembered Herman asking him what he hoped for. Mike knew solving this case would certainly lead to a promotion. He wondered how it would affect Herman.

At breakfast Bill and Matt asked why Herman was not taking part in the press conference.

Mike made the point that publicity would make it harder for him to be effective in the future.

Matt looked at Ian and quietly mouth the work "bullshit".

Ian smiled and simply said that the dancing in the spotlight was Mike's job. He said his job was done and it is time for him to move on. He made the point that there were many other problems that still need to be solved.

Bill looked at Ian as he took a sip of his coffee. He made the comment that he did not believe Ian worked for the FBI.

"Let's just say I am called on to solve the problems that are defying solution in a normal manner. I work for whoever needs my help" Ian replied.

"Well, whoever you may be, Thanks for getting to the bottom of this situation. I would have never believed anyone in my organization would have been involved in such a scheme. I will forever be in your debt," Bill said from his side of the table.

"Well, I am on the way home and that is always a treat. My wife is the best cook in the world," Ian said as he got up.

He was on the way to meet a helicopter at Montezuma Castle National Monument. It would take him all the way home and to the arms of his lovely Lesley.

"I thought he was single," Ian heard Matt say to Bill as he walked out.

Ian smiled. He had never discussed his personal life with anyone. They had reached their own conclusion.

The End

About the Author

Ronald E. Mueller

remwriter95@gmail.com

Ron grew up in what is now Flint River State Park in Southeast Iowa. The 170-year-old house Ron lived in is built into a hillside. It faces a 125-foot-high cliff towering over the little Flint River. The house and the land talked to him about; the passing of time, the struggle to conquer the land, the struggles people faced and the wonder of nature.

He climbed the cliffs, crawled into the caves, dove from the swimming rock, collected clams from the bottom of the pond, gigged and skinned frogs for their legs. He trapped muskrats for fur, hunted raccoon in the dead of night, and with only a stick hunted rabbits in the dead of winter.

His young life was outdoors, and nature tested him.

He walked to a one room stone schoolhouse uphill both ways. A stern but warm-hearted teacher, Mrs. Henry was instrumental in shaping his character as she shepherded him from the fourth to the eighth grade. A Montessori before its time. It was a great way to grow up.

His experiences inter-twined with snippets of fantasy lend themselves to the adventures he leads the reader through.

Other books by Around the World Published Authors:

The Taelo Series by Ron Mueller

Taelo: The Early Years
Taelo: The Golden Feather
Taelo: The Journey East
Taelo: Dangerous Passage
Taelo: Condor Clan Slingers

A Taelo Story by Ron Mueller
The Name of the Child
White Swan and Quiet Pheasant
Broken Spear
Floating Cloud
Quiet Rabbit
Busy Bee
Little Otter& Talking Wren
Burley Bear & Meadow Flower

A Feather-in-the-Wind Story by Ron Mueller
The Eastern Elk Clan

Science Fiction:

The Door Series:
The Door
Delivery
Journey Beyond
The Savitar Series:
Journey's End
Savitar
Confluence
Single Science Fiction:
Current Past and Future
The Door
Event Survivors
Fiction:
Alex Evercrest Series;
The River Front
The Girl on the Grill
Missing
Maggot
Imagination by Courtney Huynh and Chloe Parker

Published by: Around the World Publishing LLC.